THIS BOOK
BELONGS TO:

book sponsored by

OGDEN SCHOOL
FOUNDATION

OGDEN
SCHOOL DISTRICT

D0580566

For Logan, Quinn & Tommy,
my heart & soul & my very own
little manic monkeys.

**—R.S.**


I miss calculator watches.

**—S.C.**

No moldy sandwiches here...

ISBN 978-1-7327501-1-1

Hoarding Porter, LLC
PO Box 173
Deadwood, SD 57732

10 9 8 7 6 5 4 3 2

Printed in China

This is Porter.

She's a hoarder.

This is how you tell.

Porter's mother,
like any other,

wants her room
not to smell.

Something you need to know about Porter is that she is a little piggy who spends each day plowing through stinky piles of junk.

There's only one thing Porter
likes more than hoarding good
things and gross things.

Porter loves candy. And buried in her garbage dump of a room is a big gold coin worth three truckloads of candy.

As you may have noticed, Porter can't tell the difference between nice things and stinky piles of worthless trash.

If Porter cleans her room today and finds the gold coin, she'll get all the candy her messy little heart desires. Can you help her find it?

Can you please help her clean her room and decide what stays and what has to go?

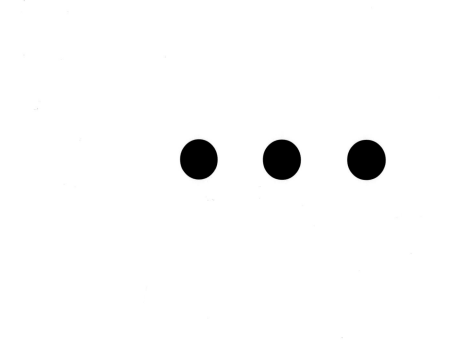

# Ready?

Let's

# GO!

Help Porter find her collection
of ten snotty handkerchiefs.
Can you find all ten?

Should she keep the 10 snotty handkerchiefs?

Help Porter find her collection
of nine remote control helicopters.
Can you find all nine?

Should she keep the 9 remote control helicopters?

YES!!

Help Porter find her collection
of eight wads of chewed-up bubble
gum. Can you find all eight?

Should she keep the 8 wads of chewed-up bubble gum?

Help Porter find her collection
of seven sparkly rings.
Can you find all seven?

Should she keep the
7 sparkly rings?

Help Porter find her collection
of six lightning-fried lizards.
Can you find all six?

Should she keep the 6 lightning-fried lizards?

Help Porter find her collection
of five manic monkeys.
Can you find all five?

Should she keep
the 5 manic
monkeys?

YES!

Help Porter find her collection
of four rotting banana peels.
Can you find all four?

Should she keep
the 4 rotting
banana peels?

NO.

Help Porter find her collection
of three shiny dump trucks.
Can you find all three?

Should she keep
the 3 shiny
dump trucks?

YES!!

Help Porter find her collection
of two moldy sandwiches.
Can you find them both?

Should she keep the
2 moldy sandwiches?

Can you help her find the gold coin so she can get her 3 truckloads of candy?

Thanks to you,
Porter's room is finally clean.

# The
# End.

# ABOUT THE AUTHOR

**SEAN COVEL** is a film and television producer who grew up in a blip of a town in the Black Hills of South Dakota. His credits include *Beneath* for Paramount Pictures, *The 12 Dogs of Christmas* directed by Academy Award Winner, Keith Merrill, and the iconic independent film, *Napoleon Dynamite*.

Together, Sean's movies have played lots of places, won a bunch of awards and whatever, and — most importantly — got nerds prom dates across the globe. He very much wishes that would've been the case when he was in high school.

Sean enjoys shooting movies, writing weirdo children's books with his weirdo friends, and lecturing at universities and film festivals internationally, but he hangs his nunchucks in Deadwood, SD.

# ABOUT THE ILLUSTRATOR

**REBECCA SWIFT** should've had a perfectly reasonable career in a perfectly reasonable field. This is due to having excellent parents. Imagine their concern as their daughter expressed interest in all things "the arts."

In addition to drawing doodles and painting pictures, Rebecca is an established singer-songwriter, having been on American Idol and releasing her first album *North of Normal* later that same year. When not art-ing up the place, Rebecca works as a professional makeup artist. Which is still art. But on faces.

Rebecca is a proud mum to two girls (Quinn and Logan) and a lil dude (Tommy). The three were in no way an inspiration for the *Porter the Hoarder* series. Except that they were. Completely. Logan has a thing for stashing candy that is borderline intervention inspiring. …It's a concern.

Rebecca hangs her many, many (many) hats in Bridgewater, SD.